COWBOY

BY BERNARD WOLF

WILLIAM MORROW & COMPANY · NEW YORK

Library of Congress Cataloging in Publication Data: Wolf, Bernard. Cowboy. Summary: Describes the life and work of Wallace McRae and his family on their ranch in Rosebud County, Montana, including the spring roundup and branding of cattle, the local rodeo, the gathering and storing of hay, and the interaction with the coal workers in town.   1. Cowboys—Montana—Rosebud County—Juvenile literature.   2. Ranch life—Montana—Rosebud County—Juvenile literature.   3. Rosebud County (Mont.)—Social life and customs—Juvenile literature.   4. McRae family—Juvenile literature.   5. Cattle trade—Montana—Rosebud County—Juvenile literature.   6. Cowboys—West (U.S.)—Juvenile literature.   7. West (U.S.)—Social life and customs—Juvenile literature.   8. Ranch life—West (U.S.)—Juvenile literature.   [1. Cowboys. 2. Ranch life—Montana.   3. Cattle trade—Montana.   4. McRae family.   5. West (U.S.)—Social life and customs]   I. Title.
F737.R95W65 1985   978.6'32   84-20541   ISBN 0-688-03877-8 | ISBN 0-688-03878-6 (lib. bdg.)

To Ruth and Wally McRae,
with affection and admiration

As far as the eye can reach, the grass moves in restless currents under a prodding wind. Small mounds of ponderosa pine relieve the monotony of the view. In midsummer, all this will be seared bone yellow by an unrelenting sun, while in winter's driving blizzard, the temperature will lock at forty degrees below zero.

Cottontails dart briefly from burrows, wrinkle their noses in wonder, then vanish. Sometimes, poised for instant flight, a pair of antelopes appear, only to disappear with a few soaring bounds. The wildflowers are tiny and carry muted colors. Life here grows small, as if not wishing to attract the punishing elements. Only the sky is big. The vast sky—like a separate world—dwarfs everything.

The land is no good for farming. A plough would peel away the fragile cover of earth only to lay bare blankets of coal. The terrain is too rough and uneven for ploughing. But native grass grows here, and even in dry times, the layers of coal beneath the surface act as natural conduits for moisture. This is fine land for raising cattle.

Wallace McRae rides his horse through a gravel pit checking pasture gates and fences on his ranch, the Rocker Six Cattle Company. His ranch is in Rosebud County, in southeastern Montana. It lies three thousand feet above sea level, part of the West's Great Northern Plains. Not long ago, the Cheyennes roamed here on their piebald ponies, feasted on plentiful game, and blessed the gods for their gifts. Now this is McRae's home and his land—all thirty thousand acres of it— his, and the bank's. While not a strict churchgoing man, he, too, is grateful for his gifts.

Tomorrow will begin one of the most important events of his year, his spring cattle roundup and branding. Not all cattle ranches are alike. McRae runs his outfit as a cow-calf operation. His year-round herd consists mostly of healthy, calf-bearing cows and good breeder bulls. Most of the calves born here are

raised until they are six months old and then sold. His outfit is not considered large by ranching standards. While thirty thousand acres seems like a lot of land, for a rancher it is a question of how many animals the land can support. After expenses and taxes, if a rancher comes away with a modest profit, he figures he's had a pretty good year. If drought and fire kill his grass and winter kills his cattle, he's lucky if he's not wiped out. It's a risky way to live, but for Wallace McRae there is no other.

In Rosebud County, there is a local history book called *They Came and Stayed*. It shows the pictures and tells the stories of the people who first came to this part of Montana and stuck it out. McRae's ancestors are in this book.

In 1882, young John B. McRae of Scotland stepped off a sailing ship in Brownsville, Texas, parting forever from the homeland that could offer him no future. He and his people had been crofters, or sharecroppers, for generations. They lived mainly by raising sheep. Now, the landowners were charging fees for the grazing of their land. Many crofter families could not pay. As a result, young sons were forced to leave and seek opportunity elsewhere.

John B. McRae dreamt of owning his own land, being his own man. America's newest western frontier was Montana, where there were few people but lots of grassland. This sounded just right to young John. Working his way North, it took him two years to reach his destination. He liked what he saw. It was a place a man could stretch out in. In spite of all adversity, he stayed.

Wallace never met John, the first McRae to settle Rosebud County, but he has heard so much about his grandfather that he feels his presence, as he feels the presence of his other ancestors. Their stories comfort him. Their experiences and problems were much the same as his own.

Now three generations of McRaes rest in the simple Lee Community Cemetery, a short distance from McRae's house. Here lie all four of his grandparents, his father and mother, a sister, aunts, uncles, and cousins. As he pulls the weeds from their gravestones, McRae silently acknowledges their gift of values. Their lives have shaped his.

By 4:30 in the morning, McRae has started his day. In the doorway of the tackroom where they store their riding equipment, stands Jon Eaton, McRae's hired hand, ready to help with the branding. Draped over one arm is a bridle with braided reins. He's ready to saddle up his horse.

Everything a cowboy wears is designed for a particular function. With the sun just above the horizon, Jon's hat provides comfortable shade for his eyes. It keeps his head cool in hot weather and warm in cold. It acts as an umbrella in rain or snow. The eagle feather is his own personal touch. There is a scarf, or "tough rag" around his throat. Blood vessels are very close to the surface of the throat, and in cold weather a cowboy's tough rag, small though it is, is one of the most important pieces of clothing he's got. His down vest, warming his torso, is fitted with snap fasteners, as is the shirt he wears under it.

A horse, suddenly startled and out of control, can hang a man up or unseat and drag him. Clothing with fasteners that pop open under stress can help prevent injuries. Strapped over his jeans and hanging half over his boots are a pair of lightweight leather chaps. They're worn to protect his legs from bad weather or sharp underbrush while riding, and burns while branding. His high-heeled leather boots provide a good anchor to the ground when he's struggling with a roped calf. On horseback, the boots' long, pointed toes help guide his feet through the stirrups' openings while the high heels secure them in place. Attached to the heels are metal spurs he presses against his horse's flanks to urge him forward.

McRae squints speculatively at the sky as he approaches the tackroom. There is a chilly tingle in the air, but not a cloud above them.

"Mornin', Wally," says Jon. "Fine day for a branding." Eyeing his boss' supply of coffee and tobacco, he adds with a grin, "Yup, you came prepared all right."

All of McRae's friends call him Wally, and though Jon Eaton is an employee, he is also one of McRae's most trusted friends. Wally values his judgment and expertise as highly as he does his own. He has consulted Jon in making many major decisions affecting the ranch.

Both men glance down the narrow county road that cuts through McRae's land. They're waiting for the arrival of Wally's neighbors. Jon leads his paint gelding from the corral as Wally follows with his gray stallion. Soon, both horses are saddled and seem as eager as the men to begin work. Down the road in a cloud of red dust, a caravan of trailer trucks appear. They brake to a stop near the corral. Already saddled horses are unloaded from their trailers while the men greet one another.

No rancher can run an outfit without help. On really big ranches, owners can pay for large crews of year-round hands. Wally can only afford one. A few of his neighbors can manage two. But when the work requires more manpower, these independent ranchers help one another. Today, neighbors help Wally with his roundup and branding; soon, he will help them.

The riders head out across the range toward McRae's winter pasture, taking pleasure in the morning and the company. By inviting his neighbors to ride his land during roundup and branding, Wally is telling them that he trusts them. Should he become seriously injured, their familiarity with his land would help his neighbors locate and rescue him, and it could help them prevent the spread of a fire on his ranch during the hot, dry summers.

The sun is still low above the eastern horizon. Early morning is the best time

of day for a roundup because it is coolest then. The cattle will be trailed a long distance to the branding corral, and a roundup during the heat of the day would tire them unnecessarily.

When the men arrive at his winter pasture, the riders fan out. They will try to

gather about a third of the cattle that have wintered here. The pasture is fairly close to McRae's house so that in cold weather he can haul extra feed to his animals over the shortest possible distance. But the pasture itself is huge and it takes time to gather up and form the animals into a group. The gate to the branding corral is opened at Wally's signal and the animals surge through in a straggly column. There are two riders on either side at the front. As the herd moves out, two more ease their horses alongside the middle of the column. Jon Eaton and one of Wally's cousins, Doug McRae, ride drag behind the herd, eating its dust. Whistling softly, they move the herd at a steady pace, yet slow enough so the newborn calves can keep up. In all, Wally reckons they'll be branding about one hundred seventy-five calves today. This number will allow the men to finish their work more quickly, while it is still cool, and it will make it easier to match each calf with its mother after branding. An unweaned calf that is separated from its mother will not usually survive.

As they approach the corral, McRae is pleased once more by the height and richness of the grass on his land. Few people understand that the crop he raises on his ranch isn't cattle; it's grass. The cattle harvest the grass, a renewable resource not used by humans, and convert it into protein in the form of beef. But the land on which the grass grows is an expensive factory. In fact, it's Wally's single greatest expense. Each month, year-round, payments for the land must be made to the bank. Also, two or three tractors (at $15,000 apiece) are needed to put up hay in summer. Other costly machines are needed to form the hay so that it can be moved to the cattle in winter. Property taxes are high. Income taxes are high. Jon Eaton's salary must be paid. Finally, there is Wally's own time and labor. The expenses involved in raising the cattle must be deducted from their sale price. Sometimes there's a profit. McRae figures it's worth it. He's earned the freedom to live his life in a way that's right for him. He'll settle for that.

All the cattle are inside the branding corral and bunched against its far end. Wally's neighbor Jack Bradley is here. After checking to see that everyone else is in position, he mounts up. Jack will be first roper today. That's a compliment to his skill. Nobody seems to be watching him, but everyone is. Bradley is a top hand. That's the highest praise a cowboy can earn. It means that every job he does, he does right. He gets no extra pay or reward for this other than his neighbors' respect.

Bradley nudges his horse softly into the herd. In his left hand, he holds the coils of his nylon rope together with his horse's bridle reins. With his right hand, he begins to build a loop in his lariat. He points his horse's head at the calf he has selected. Swinging his lariat, he throws the loop sidearmed so that it lands

just in front of the calf's hind legs. When the calf steps forward, Bradley jerks up hard on his rope, closing the noose around the animal's legs. Then he makes some quick wraps with his rope around his saddle horn, turns his horse, and drags the calf away from the herd to where the calf "wrasslers" are waiting.

McRae's calf wrasslers are not cowboys nor even permanent residents of the rural community. They are high-school boys from the nearby town of Colstrip.

Wally likes to hire these town kids because he feels it betters their understanding of what he and his neighbors do, while giving them a chance to earn some money and participate in the excitement of a branding. What they lack in expertise, they make up for with enthusiasm.

It takes two wrasslers to handle a calf. They must be well-coordinated and fast. Technique is more important than strength. When the roper drags the calf toward them, one wrassler grabs the animal's tail while the second pulls back on the rope attached to its hind leg, lifting it off balance. Then, both wrasslers jerk hard, tripping the animal on its side to the ground. One wrassler releases the calf's tail and grips its top front leg, lifting it up so that it can't rise from the

ground. The other wrassler frees the rope, grabs the animal's top hind leg, stretching it taut and exposing its left hip. He braces himself with his foot against the calf's bottom leg. Now the calf is ready for branding.

Each spring, all new calves must receive an ownership mark or brand. This prevents disputes between neighbors, and it prepares the animals for eventual sale. In the old days, branding irons were heated over wood fires, a slow and inefficient method. Today, cowboys use propane-fueled fires.

With steady hands, the cowboy presses the hot end of the branding iron to the calf's hip. Then he leans on it, just so. Instantly, there is a hiss, a white billow of smoke and the pungent scent of burnt hide. When he lifts the iron, the Rocker Six brand is clearly and permanently embedded in the calf's rump.

While still on the ground, each calf is vaccinated against black leg disease;

without the vaccine, they would die. On all heifers (female calves), Wally has a piece of skin cut so that it flaps down from the animal's lower jaw. In winter, it isn't always possible to read an animal's brand from a distance. This skin flap or "wattle" stands out clearly in silhouette. His neighbors all use different marks of identification, in addition to branding, on their cattle. Finally, ear tagging makes it easier to count how many calves have been branded.

As the branding irons burn into their hides, the calves bawl with fear and pain, but as soon as they are released, they scamper back to their mothers in the herd with no sign of discomfort. If anything, it is the vaccine injection that makes them wobbly.

Wally is the cutter. He's an expert. During every spare moment this morning, he's been honing the edge of his knife on a whetstone till it's razor sharp. He hovers over each bull calf as it is being branded, his knife hand held high. Then he stoops down swiftly and castrates the animal by removing the testes. Now the bull calf is a steer. This alteration makes male cattle more docile, increases their potential for gaining weight, and enables a rancher to be highly selective in shaping his herd's more desirable genetic traits. But great care must be taken. As cutter, Wally washes his hands and knife in surgical disinfectant before castrating every bull calf. His most important concern is that no animal become sick.

During branding, bull calves' horns, if they have any, are cut off to prevent them from injuring other animals when they are mature. Jon Eaton handles this job. With the very young bull calves, he burns their horn buds out of their heads with a straight, hot iron.

Wally and the other men working with him are keenly aware that the animals they handle are suffering pain and trauma. How much pain they don't know. They hope that by doing their jobs quickly and expertly, they can keep any suffering to a minimum. All these procedures are essential to raising a productive herd of cattle. There are no easier ways. As McRae points out, "Any cowboy worth a damn does what he does because he likes animals, not because he enjoys hurting them."

By eleven-thirty, the sun is high and hot, the last of the new calves have been branded. What remains to be done is to vaccinate the two-year-old heifers and put a year brand on them. Since these animals are much too big to wrestle to the ground, they are prodded single file through a squeeze chute. Wally waits with the tailgate rope in his right hand and the collar lever in his left. As a heifer approaches the chute, he drops the rope closing the tailgate behind her, prevent-

ing her from backing out. When the heifer reaches the end of the chute, he pulls the lever and a headcatch or collar closes around the animal's neck, restricting her movement. One cowboy injects her with the serum she will need every year for the rest of her life. Another puts a brand on her shoulder that tells when she was born.

When the last heifer passes through the squeeze chute, the day's branding is completed. The corral gate is opened, and all the animals are driven out to a large holding pasture. Wally counts the cows as they pass by to get an idea of how many they've gathered and handled this day. The animals are moving pretty quickly, so he uses a fence post as a fixed point of reference and counts them two at a time as they reach this point.

It's been a productive, strenuous morning. All hands can relax now. This is a good time to swap observations on the day's events. Appetites are sharp, but

no one mentions their hunger. As though on cue, a cloud of dust appears down the road. It's Wally's pickup. Ruth McRae and their two teenage daughters are bringing lunch. It is tradition that the host feeds his neighbors during roundup and branding.

This is a festive time. For a cowboy, roundup and branding represents the most important cultural event of the year.

With lunch finished, Wally's neighbors load their horses into trailers and head back to their own outfits. Some will return to help with tomorrow's roundup. Others will come in place of those who cannot. But Wally and Jon Eaton can't call it a day yet. Their next task is to move the breeding bulls from their winter

pastures to the pastures where the cows and heifers will be spending the summer. This begins the mating season. Care must be taken to match smaller bulls with the young heifers and the larger males with mature cows. The rest is left to Mother Nature. In about nine months, Wally will have a new crop of calves. Now, he and Jon can relax and turn toward home.

When Jon and Wally unsaddle and unbridle their horses, Wally's horse, Owl, immediately trots over to the soft earth lot in the corral and scuffs the ground a little bit. Then he sinks to his front knees, rolls over onto his back and swings

from one side to the other in pure bliss, stirring a cloud of dust around him. He's been ridden pretty hard today, worked up a sweat and an itch. Now, he knows his work's done, and this is a fine way to scratch and stretch at the same time. A moment later, he's on his haunches. With a mighty toss of his mane, he shakes the dust from his body, scrambles to his feet, and goes off looking for something to eat.

Wally glances again with pleasure at the carpet of blue-green grass wherever he turns. All is well at the Rocker Six Cattle Company. It's been a good day.

The following Sunday, it is raining, but it doesn't matter. The McRaes rarely work on Sunday. Ruth and their daughters drive into Colstrip to go to church while Wally remains at home puttering around the house. In the afternoon, a car pulls into the driveway. Wally is delighted with an unexpected visit from his son, Clint. Clint is working as a cowboy for the Padlock Ranch, one of the largest in Montana. The rain has brought the huge roundup and branding on the Padlock to a standstill. The ground, turned to slippery mud, would be hazardous to men and beasts. Clint's boss gave him the afternoon off. He's been working outdoors for weeks while living in a sleeping bag and tent.

Wally sits quietly, listening with keen attention to his son's tales. His back curved like a bowstring, he methodically sharpens his cutting knife on a whetstone. He is proud of his son who, at nineteen, has grown into a competent, tough young man. He hopes that Clint will run the Rocker Six one day when Wally is too old. But Clint thinks he would like to be an artist. He has talent and Wally has agreed that he should pursue his potential in that field when he goes to college in the fall.

Later in the day, the weather changes. The clouds vanish and there is a brilliant sunset. On Monday and Tuesday, Wally is able to complete his roundup and branding.

The Forsyth Horse Show is the oldest in Montana and one of the oldest in the West. It started in 1947. The McRae family has been involved with it from its beginning, and as far back as a lot of people can remember, Wally McRae has been the show's announcer.

The town of Forsyth, the only real town close by, is about an hour's drive from Wally's ranch. Each spring, he donates his time, talent, and sound equipment to this show free of charge. With his remarkable speaking voice and his knowledge of each event, his services are in demand for commercial horseshows and rodeos around the state. He's a one-man show himself, making announcements, exhorting the participants, cracking jokes, and playing the appropriate music for the action on the field.

The Forsyth show is popular because it combines a horse show with a rodeo.

Most of the animals entered are working horses used on ranches. During the three-day show, some owners enter their horses in twenty or more events.

The barrel race is a competition for women riders. The contestants run a cloverleaf pattern around three barrels. It's a timed event that demonstrates a horse's agility in racing around the barrels without touching or knocking them over, then sprinting for the finish line as quickly as possible. If a barrel is over-

turned, there's a five-point penalty and no chance at winning the prize money.

A young calf comes speeding out of the chute with a cowboy in hot pursuit. The rider twirls his looped lariat above his head. With exact timing and precision, he throws his rope so that the noose floats over and in front of the calf's neck. As soon as the animal runs into the opening, the noose closes; in a flash, the cowboy wraps the rope around his saddle horn, leaps off his horse, and runs to the side of the calf, wrassling him to the ground. The horse takes up the slack on the rope and prevents the calf from rising. Now, the cowboy swiftly ties three of the animal's legs together and throws his hands up. This signals the judges to stop their watches and announce his time.

The rodeo events are always crowd pleasers. When the chute opens and some daring cowboy comes charging out on top of a half-crazed bucking bronc, people have to wonder how any horse could have so many moves in him. These are "spoiled" horses that would never allow themselves to be saddle broken. Their owners sell them to rodeo producers.

"This cowboy's got it made!" exclaims Wally. "Hang in there, pardner!"

Another cowboy is bounced around like a Ping-Pong ball on his barebacked bronc. All he's got to hang on to—with one hand—is a sort of suitcase handle attached to a rigging that runs around the animal's flanks. The rider has to stay seated for eight seconds while encouraging his bronc to buck as hard as possible. This cowboy has got determination, but the devil he's riding has other ideas.

The next rider doesn't even do as well. He's positioned poorly and knows he'll never make his eight-second ride. So does his crazy-eyed bronc, who lunges forward, then jerks back and watches with satisfaction as his rider goes sailing over his head. The horse jumps over the downed cowboy and races toward the open corral gate. Even when they are upset, horses usually avoid trampling or stepping on people on the ground. No one seems sure why.

Rodeo contestants come from a variety of backgrounds. Some come from ranching families. Some are college students. They work at a variety of different jobs. All enjoy the dangers and challenges of rodeo competition. It's a macho thing to do. Bruises, torn ligaments, broken bones, and wrenched collars all come with the territory. But these cowboys are tough. They have to be.

In any rodeo, bull riding is the most dangerous event. A bull is almost impossible to ride. When a rider is thrown from a bucking bronc, the horse just wants to run away. When a rider is thrown off a bull, the bull's only desire is to kill. Sometimes, they are successful. More often, they are diverted from their intended targets by the antics of nimble rodeo clowns who draw the bull's attention away from a thrown rider to themselves. But Wally has seen quite a number of

contestants "get an egg broke in 'em, bad." Bucking bulls are bred for their athletic ability, their meanness, and their hatred for people. This huge beast is a good example. The crowd gasps as he does a complete, aerial turnabout before jolting to the ground again. The only thing keeping this cowboy on the animal's back is balance and strength. There's no natural place to ease his body into. He's got guts, too—he needs that to keep his ride going eight seconds.

"He's gonna make it folks," says Wally. "A fine ride, and—oh, oh! Look out, cowboy!" he exclaims. The crowd sucks in its breath. With a savage ripple of its muscular back, the bull has thrown its rider a few feet away—much too close for comfort. There isn't time or space for the clown to distract him. Head lowered, he bears down on the cowboy like an express locomotive. On pure reflex, the injured rider lifts himself off the ground and, forgetting pain, sprints for the nearest fence. Then, at the last moment, he makes an impossible head-first leap over the barrier just inches ahead of the bull's awesome impact.

Wally clears his throat in relief. He's not the only one.

While the cutting competition is one of the less popular events of the show, for ranchers and cowhands it is an absorbing spectacle of skill and grace. The object is to demonstrate a horse's ability to enter a herd of cattle, cut an animal out, and hold it out of the herd for as long as possible. Two other riders hold the herd in place. The cutter, cautiously entering the herd, points out to his horse the animal he wants by using rein signals and shifting his weight in the saddle. From this point on, the rider just sits there and the horse takes charge of bringing the animal out of the herd. These horses are extraordinary. Once a calf is separated from the herd, they move with catlike agility, sensing beforehand the animal's every attempt to return to the herd and blocking each effort to do so.

On the third and final day of the show, it isn't until late in the afternoon that someone hands Wally a note. He reads it, then, with a grin, he announces, "May I have your attention please? Folks, I've just been informed that we now have nine very brave—or very loco—volunteers for our last event. Looks like we're gonna get our wild horse race after all!"

There are hoots of laughter and anticipation. People hurry away from the food concession booths back to their seats. Nobody wants to miss this.

Down the track comes a rider. Before him, on a long rope and wearing a halter, is a screaming demon of a horse, lashing the air in rage with his front hooves. Behind the rider there are two others, each with a wild horse on a rope in front of him. These are wild range animals never broken to ride and unused to all human contact.

Waiting with mixed emotions at the center of the track are three teams of three men. Each volunteer has a title. One is the anchorman; he's usually big and heavy and it's his job to hold the horse by the rope attached to its halter. The mugger approaches the horse and restrains him by gripping the animal's ears. The third man is the rider. He helps hold the horse until the mugger has a firm grip. Then, the mugger holds the horse while the anchorman and rider put a saddle on him.

It's a wild scene with men and horses falling every which way. One team isn't doing too badly, though. They've got their horse saddled, and sure enough, the rider is mounting up! With his feet secure in the stirrups, he nods to his teammates to let the animal go, and then all hell breaks loose! Never having been ridden before, this horse knows nothing about riding signals and couldn't care less. He just wants out and starts running like the wind—only in the wrong direction.

The crowd is screaming with laughter.

The racetrack is a half-mile around. The first rider to complete one full circuit wins the race. But how to get this crazy horse to turn?

Meanwhile, a second rider is mounted and speeding down the track the right way. He's looking good—looking very good—and he's almost halfway around the track now.

The first rider's pulling with all his strength to turn his horse's head when, without losing a stride, the animal leaps over the track fence and speeds across the inner field toward distant pastures, his rider holding on for dear life.

Within sight of the finish line, rider number two suddenly finds himself launched into space. His horse just comes to an instant stop.

Now, thundering around the final bend comes rider number one, determination etched on his face, every muscle stretched taut—thirty yards . . . twenty . . . ten—and he crosses the finish line to the shouts and cheers of the spectators!

The Forsyth show over, Wally and Jon Eaton respond to a call from Wally's cousin Duke to help him with the roundup and branding. Duke's place is the ranch where Wally grew up, but things are different now. As they work, they can clearly see signs of the bitter conflict that has torn their community apart for more than a decade and threatens their very way of life.

The West may have changed, but the good guys and the bad guys remain. The bad guys don't wear guns anymore. They don't need to.

For hours, the men in the branding corral have been assaulted by the awful, nonstop mechanical racket nearby. This portion of Duke McRae's land lies adjacent to the Rosebud Mine, the largest strip coal mine in the world. Looming above the range like a prehistoric monster is one of the mine's four dragline machines. Weighing six million pounds each, they are so complex that they must be assembled from thousands of parts right on the spot where they will be used.

The dragline operates on a long, movable boom. A steel cable, passing over the tip of the boom, supports a bucket that can scoop up and dump material to either side. The buckets are the size of one-car garages. In the Rosebud Mine, they are used to strip away the overburden, or mantle of earth, expos-

ing the coal seams beneath. The drag-lines never sleep. Each can move about sixty-five thousand tons of earth in a day. At night, they work with the aid of high-intensity lights and when they must be moved, they walk on gargan-tuan, stublike feet.

From time to time, the ground shud-ders for miles around from the shock waves of explosives in the mine, either blasting a newly exposed coal seam or loosening a very large section of the overburden. When the coal dust settles, there is a waiting line of large trucks. A huge coal-shoveling machine thrusts its jaws into the blasted coal seam. After two or three mighty gulps and disgorg-ings, each truck is fully loaded. They move out of the mine, carrying the coal to the power plant nearby. The trucks return to the mine for more coal. There is no sign of human life in the mine; only the army of machines—busy day and night—beeping and clanking.

Across Montana and throughout the Great Northern Plains, other mining operations are in progress. Some are for coal, some for rare metals and minerals. They are expanding, yet no one knows what permanent change or damage they are effecting on the environment. The coal hauled out of Rosebud Mine contains twenty-five percent water. For years, ranchers, scientists, and conservationists have struggled to prove to the state government that once the coal is removed, the land becomes useless for livestock production. Taking away the coal removes the natural conductor of water, which regulates and sustains the growth of grass on the thin overburden. The mining companies point with pride to their program of reclaiming disturbed land and restoring it to what they say is "close" to its original condition. But since this land has never been used to graze cattle, no one really knows how effective the program is.

The ranching families who must regularly drive into Colstrip can't avoid the ugly reality that no amount of wishing will remove. Soaring five hundred-seven feet into the sky are the smokestacks of units one and two of the Colstrip power plant. A third stack, rising nearly seven hundred feet, has just been erected for what will be generating unit three, and next to it, the massive hulk of the generator for unit four. This is what coal mining is all about.

In 1958, the Northern Pacific Railroad stopped producing coal for its steam locomotives, and Colstrip became a ghost town with just a post office, a school, and a few houses as reminders of better days. The following year, Montana Power Company bought the coal leases, the Colstrip townsite, and mining equipment from the railroad. Colstrip would be a perfect site for a major power plant. There were those ranchers who believed that the construction of a power plant would bring great new prosperity to this area and would benefit everyone. Many sold all or part of the land they owned for huge sums of money. Some went to work for the power company. Families and friends were estranged as they disagreed over whether or not the power plant should be built. In the end, the power company had its way. Colstrip unit one became operational in 1975 and unit two a year later. Nothing here has been the same since.

Each generating unit burns two hundred tons of powdered coal per hour. The coal converts to steam and the steam to electricity—and noise. From any part of Colstrip, at any hour, can be heard a steady howling from the bowels of the earth; the sound made by the giant fans inside the smokestacks as they suction burnt coal debris up the funnels and into the air.

To put a stop to further pollution, Wally McRae and a handful of ranchers led a fierce battle against the construction of Colstrip units three and four. The law found their cause just and halted construction. Suddenly, there were a lot of construction workers out of jobs. The court reversed its decision, the men went back to work, and units three and four began to grow. For Wally and the other ranchers, it was a bitter defeat. But they would gladly fight the battle again.

Ruth McRae is a quiet, gentle, and very private person; she's devoutly religious yet down-to-earth. Ruth and Wally first met on a blind date that they both tried to cancel. He was a Navy lieutenant in Norfolk, Va. She was a nurse. When they decided to marry, Ruth had only a vague idea of what a ranch was or where Montana might be.

In the evening as she is preparing supper, Ruth takes a phone call for Wally. A group of high school history teachers from different parts of Montana are coming to Colstrip tomorrow to see first-hand what is happening there. They would like Wally and Bill Gillen, another rancher, to give their views as permanent residents and representatives of the agricultural community.

Late the next afternoon, Wally, Bill, and the visiting teachers squeeze into one of the rooms in Colstrip's only motel. It's crowded and stuffy. The teachers are tired and dusty but alert.

They've just completed two long guided tours of the mine and the power plant, and they've been given the full VIP treatment. Now they're eager to hear what Bill and Wally have to say.

"They put on a pretty good show, don't they?" Wally grins.

"Well, those stacks *are* impressive," says one woman.

"Absolutely," agrees Bill. "Biggest things in Rosebud County. They've also caused the first serious air pollution this county's ever had."

"All I saw coming out the top of the stacks was some thin, white vapor," says another man. "It looked clean to me."

"That's right," Bill replies. "It is. Now. But this is summer. Except for air conditioning, most people don't use much power now. They spend a lot of time outdoors. But you come back when it's cold. Go on up to the Northern

Cheyenne reservation. If the conditions are right, you'll see a blanket of gray junk just hanging in the sky for days as far as you can look."

Wally stubs out one cigarette and lights another. "I guess what bothers me most is the senseless waste of it," he says. A major power plant was never needed in Colstrip. They picked the wrong place. They should have built it in California. That's where the biggest demand for power is. The funny part is, if the power company *had* gone that way, they'd be making the big profits they'll never see in Colstrip."

"Why is that?" the teacher asks.

"Because their operation here is wastefully inefficient. Between here and the West Coast it's mostly open country where there's not much need for power, so the electricity generated in Colstrip has to travel a very long distance. By the time it gets to the cities where the demand is high, about seventy percent is lost through power-line falloff."

The room is silent as this sinks in. Then, a lady says, "But isn't the power company here because the coal's here and they can produce energy cheaply?"

"Sure, the coal's here," Wally agrees. "But how cheap is the power when it has to be sent long distance to the people who want it? If the coal were hauled to a coastal plant and converted there, it would actually make the production of energy cheaper, less wasteful and more profitable."

Wally's voice is hoarse as he concludes: "In thirty years, Colstrip won't even exist anymore, economically. By then, the power plant will be too old and expensive to operate. There probably won't be enough coal left to fuel the plant, anyway. All the workers will have gone, chasing after other rainbows. We'll be left to live with the mess. And all for what? What will have been accomplished?"

In the morning, Wally's brother-in-law, Kent Montgomery, comes to the Rocker Six to help Wally cut studs and brand yearling colts. He's brought his brother, Lynn, and one of his sons as well. After Ruth's bountiful lunch, the men move off to Kent's outfit to do more of the same.

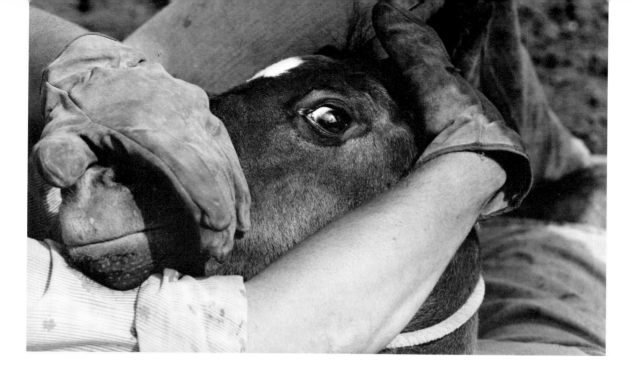

The technique of cutting and branding young horses isn't much different from
what is done with calves. But yearling colts and older breeding stallions despise
being touched or handled in any way. They'll fight furiously when they are
roped. As usual, Wally is the cutter—if the other two can ever bring this stud to
the ground. For five minutes, Kent and Lynn have had a rope on him but
haven't been able to take him down. Wally keeps a respectful distance. He
doesn't want a flying hoof for dessert. Then, with a coordinated yank on the
rope, the young horse comes falling to the ground. Immediately, Wally grabs the
animal's head until Kent's hired hand, Floyd, can get his arms around the horse's
lower jaw to steady him. Now, Kent and Lynn tie the stud's back legs together
and raise one leg higher than the other. This prevents the animal from injuring

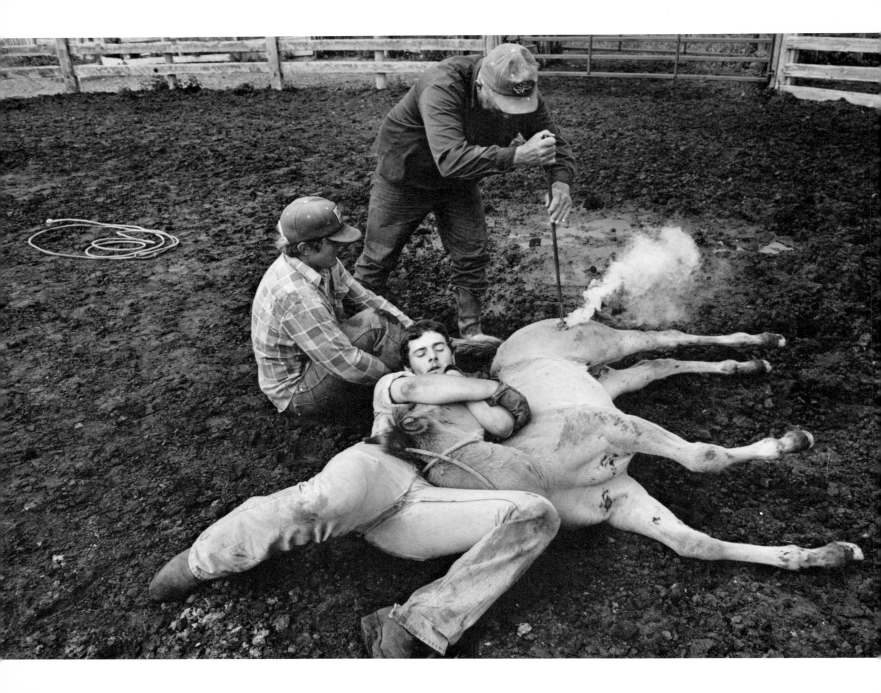

itself while giving Wally enough room to cut. All this is done as gently as possible. No cowboy would ever harm a horse; they are too fond of them.

Most of the horses cowboys ride are geldings and make fine saddle horses. They train well and are easy to handle. Only a few colts are left unaltered. Those are males who have the potential to grow into good, breeding stallions.

As with calves, putting a brand on a colt is a mark of ownership. If anything, these young horses react even more fiercely to being handled than the stallions. Because their hides are thinner than a calf's, the branding iron used is smaller, cooler, and requires less pressure when it's applied.

From the other side of the corral, the colt's mother watches and whinnies anxiously. In a moment, her baby is on his feet and scampering toward the open gate to rejoin her. The men smile. For a cowboy, horses are one of God's more beautiful ideas.

A few years ago, some people in town formed an amateur theater group. They called it The Coal and Cattle Country Players.

"Yeah," Wally laughs, "I'm the only cattle country there. All the others come from coal."

Nevertheless, he joined the group. One reason was a desire to improve communications between the ranchers and the coal workers. The other reason is that he's a remarkably gifted, natural actor who is completely at ease on a stage and enjoys every minute of it.

Each summer, the group puts on a melodrama in Colstrip's high school auditorium. This one is titled "The Shame of Tombstone." In it Wally plays the part of the oldtimer. He hasn't shaved for weeks and really looks like an old desert

rat. From the moment the curtain parts, the plot is almost always predictable. The sight gags and punch lines are outrageously corny but are delivered so earnestly by all the players that the audience is convulsed with laughter. For final satisfaction (with a little help from the oldtimer), the villain gets his in the end. For once, ranchers and townspeople have gathered together to share and enjoy a community achievement.

Before Wally McRae's ancestors first settled in Rosebud County, long before the coal and power companies took hold of the land, the Indians of the Great Plains were here. Although today's Plains tribes live on government-managed land, Indian delegations still gather to celebrate a common heritage and honor sacred traditions. It is the annual powpow.

From the campgrounds outside the Northern Cheyenne reservation comes the beating of drums and the singing of ancient songs. Among the Plains tribes here there are a few, even today, who still remember the old stories as they were told to them by their fathers when they were young. Now they tell it to their grandchildren. It is a terrible tale, but one that should be heard:

"Once, in a different time, the earth was bed, protector, and provider. The buffalo, the antelope, and the deer covered the land like a blanket. The streams ran pure, the fish were plentiful, and there was no hunger. There was peace between brothers for the people were content.

"Soon there were many wagon trains. With them came men who wished to build roads on the land. They sent buffalo hunters who killed hundreds of animals only for their skins. The meat was left to rot. Even the prairie dogs could not gorge so much.

"The Great Father in Washington sent chiefs with treaties that promised no one would disturb the people or their land without consent. They lied. The white men no longer asked for what they wanted. What they could not get by consent, they stole or took by force.

"Chief of the Bluecoats was The Long-haired Thief who stole many horses from the people. The Bluecoats called him Custer. He was a cruel man, full of hatred, who cherished the making of death. The chiefs of the Plains people joined forces. Together, their warriors surprised The Long-haired Thief and his men at the Valley of the Greasy Grass (Little Bighorn), and the killing was terrible to see. The Long-haired Thief died hard. Most of his men died, too.

"It was a great victory, but great suffering followed. Waves of Bluecoats came to kill everyone—and nearly did. They took the people's lives, but what they

really wanted was their land. In the end, they took that too. The heart breaks to speak of it."

General George Armstrong Custer was given a hero's funeral, but some records have called these events the most shameful in American history.

The Elders speak and those assembled here listen with respect and thoughtfulness—even the very young who do not understand. Children play happily in the golden afternoon. They disturb no one. There is good, home-cooked food here. Everywhere, there are people in their finest buckskins, beads, jewels, and feathers. In the next days, the tribal chiefs will discuss mutual concerns. There will be feasting and religious ceremonies. But in the evenings and far, far into the night, there will be dancing, and the night will embrace their joyful gift.

The sun is broiling, the dust is into everything, and Wally McRae and Jon Eaton are cussing with conviction. This job's too much like farming. But it can't be put off any longer. The haying's got to be done before the weather gets too dry.

Jon is operating the tractor that cuts the grass, while Wally drives the tractor that pulls the hay-stacking machine. This device is like a big vacuum cleaner that sucks up the cut grass and forms it into stacks, then deposits them on the ground. It's sweaty, irritating work. What makes it worse is that the grass often gets caught between gears or another mechanical part and something either breaks or jams. Sure enough, one of Wally's controls freezes, and he jams on the brake, swearing. Allison, his seventeen-year-old daughter, climbs to the top of the stacking machine. A lot of grass has blown up here, and if left it would become too dirty or moldy, so Al-

lison throws it onto the ground to be gathered later. Meanwhile, Wally tries to locate the source of his problem. With relief, he finds that nothing's broken, just clogged up.

Nothing lasts forever. Not even this miserable job. It's late in the day when Wally and Jon climb out of their tractors. But before them lie the fruits of their labor. The grass has been good this year. The winter will be less difficult.

Some evenings, when the weather is fine, Wally likes to go out walking on the land, just for the pure pleasure of it. There's always so much to see: sometimes a fresh wildflower; or maybe an old Indian bead from someone long ago. Words are not enough to say what he feels.

"God," Wally murmurs. "God, how I love it!"